JE

A PORTRAIT OF SPOTTED DEER'S GRANDFATHER

Amy Littlesugar
Illustrated by Marlowe deChristopher

Albert Whitman & Company · Morton Grove, Illinois

FOREWORD

GEORGE CATLIN (1796–1872) gave up a successful career as a portrait painter in Philadelphia to pursue a lifelong dream unlike that of any white man before him: to capture on canvas the great Indian tribes of the American West before the old ways of their people vanished forever.

In 1832, accompanied by grizzled fur trappers, he ventured two thousand miles up the Missouri on the riverboat *Yellowstone*, into a wilderness yet untouched by homesteaders and wagon trains. There he painted the portraits of Crow, Blackfoot, Assiniboin, and other Plains peoples. He made quick pen-and-ink sketches as well, of buffalo hunts, camp life, and sacred rituals which few white men had ever seen.

Painting at a furious rate, he spent the next five years creating an enormous pictorial history of over fifty native tribes. (About four hundred fifty of these pictures are housed in the Smithsonian Institution's National Museum of American Art.)

But 1836 marked George Catlin's last trip west of the Mississippi. In August, he headed north toward Minnesota, to find the legendary pipestone quarry where many tribes went to carve their ceremonial pipes.

Along the way, he observed villages of Woodland people, among them the gracious Chippewa. It was a gathering time. The women picked and dried berries for the winter to come, the men speared and smoked fish, and children tended the gardens of corn, beans, and pumpkins. This story imagines that visit, and the very different individuals he might have encountered.

In writing this book, I went on a journey of my own, discovering many things about George Catlin and the people he painted. I learned that he was less than perfect, both as an artist and as a man, but that his deep respect for the first Americans, in a world that was rapidly changing, never wavered. More than one hundred fifty years later, his admiration and sympathy speak to us through the portraits.

Warriors, mothers, medicine men, and elder chiefs. These bold images still look back, much as I imagined Moose Horn might have done—with pride and dignity.

Catlin, George. *Male Caribou, a Brave, 1836.*

IT WAS 1836, IN THE LAST DAYS OF
THE BEAVER. A SHAMAN OF MANY
SPIRIT HELPERS FORETOLD THE
COMING OF A GREAT WHITE VISITOR.
IT WOULD BE THE MEDICINE
PAINTER, GEORGE CATLIN.

HE WOULD JOURNEY BY CANOE
UP THE ST. PETER'S RIVER TO
SPEND THE TIME OF THE HARVEST
MOON IN THE CAMP OF THE
CHIPPEWA. HE WOULD COME
ESPECIALLY TO PAINT THE PORTRAIT
OF SPOTTED DEER'S GRANDFATHER,
MOOSE HORN, WHO WAS ONCE A
FAMOUS WARRIOR.

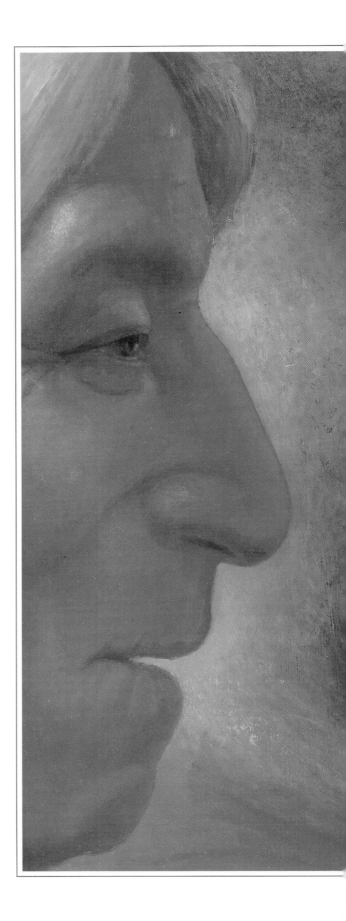

Spotted Deer loved hearing stories about his grandfather. Tonight, as they sat before the wigwam, he could imagine him as a young man, tall and straight, wearing his purple war belt and the red sash with the eagle feather.

"Grandfather," he said, "you are so handsome. On the Medicine Painter's canvas cloth you would live forever!"

But Moose Horn was not so sure.

"Why should an old man give away his face?" he asked. "If I give my face to the Medicine Painter, he may take my spirit. If I lose my spirit, I will not be able to find my way to the village of the western sky one day."

The next day, Spotted Deer and his two uncles went to wait for the Medicine Painter at the river. Spotted Deer wore new moccasins, and his mother had braided his hair that morning, rubbing it with tallow until it shone.

"Maybe the Medicine Painter will make a picture of *you*," teased

his uncles. But Spotted Deer shook his head. It was his grandfather's face he longed to see on the canvas cloth.

Soon a canoe appeared on the horizon. Closer and closer it came, until one uncle shouted, "It is he! The Medicine Painter!"

Spotted Deer's heart hammered in his chest. He saw a small white man dressed in buckskin. His eyes were the color of blue water.

Spotted Deer's uncles strode down to the bank. They greeted George Catlin and his companion. Then, as Spotted Deer watched, his uncles helped Catlin unload his canoe.

Spotted Deer did not know where to look first. He saw a three-legged stand, smooth as slippery elm; "sketching books," like thin

sheets of birchbark; and the painting colors themselves, which were
stored in the bladders of fish.

Then Spotted Deer noticed the magic brushes. Of all the Medicine
Painter's treasures, these were the most wonderful. On the way back
to the village, he could not take his eyes off them. Click, clack, click,
clack, they went in the canvas pouch that George Catlin carried.

Meanwhile, Spotted Deer's family had set out to change Moose Horn's mind. But it was not going to be easy. Up before the dogs on this day of the Medicine Painter's coming, he paced and paced.

Spotted Deer's mother came to brush Moose Horn's silvery hair with a bundle of stiff grass. She said softly, "Father-in-law, the white Medicine Painter is said to have painted the face of the Grand Pawnee, Horse Chief."

Spotted Deer's sisters, who were mending the porcupine quills of Moose Horn's shirt, said, "Grandfather, Mandan girls have smiled for the Medicine Painter, too."

And Spotted Deer's father reminded Moose Horn that in the camp of the Blackfoot, the Medicine Painter had seen the calling of the priests to a dying man. "Few white men have ever been known to do that," he said.

Still Moose Horn was not convinced. Not even when Spotted Deer and his uncles returned with George Catlin, and the people greeted him warmly. Not even that night around the fire, when the red stone pipe was passed in peace.

Across the circle of men so that George Catlin could hear, Moose Horn muttered, "Why should an old man give away his face?"

Yet in the morning, Moose Horn followed the Medicine Painter to the edge of the village. There, he watched as George Catlin painted the river birch and the ancient pines. He painted the women laughing and talking as they knelt in their gardens, and the sleeping babies standing in their cradleboards.

Faster and faster his brushes flew, as though what he saw might disappear when he looked again.

Moose Horn began to think, "The Medicine Painter is like the rock. He sits and sees."

Then, late in the day, George Catlin made another picture—
a portrait. It was the face of a woman so old it was said she could
remember a time when butterflies played with children. That was
a time before the white man came and fished the rivers, hunted the
forests, and plowed the earth.

Moose Horn looked into the Medicine Painter's eyes and was surprised. He saw sadness there, a sadness he understood too well. "Our world is changing fast," he thought. "Too fast even for the Medicine Painter's magic brushes."

That night in their wigwam, Moose Horn lay down beside
Spotted Deer as he had done since the boy was very small. Tonight,
though, he had no song to sing or story to tell. His thoughts were
far away.

"Please, Grandfather," begged Spotted Deer, "won't you sit down for the Medicine Painter?"

Moose Horn smiled at his grandson. "You must sleep now," he said gently, "and not think of such things."

Soon Spotted Deer was asleep. Moose Horn rose and went to sit beneath the stars. A soft breeze stirred in the ironwood trees.

The spirits are restless tonight, thought Moose Horn. *Like me.* He pulled his blanket closer. His eyes felt heavy.

When he looked again, a young warrior stood before him. He wore Moose Horn's purple war belt and the red sash with the eagle feather. Moose Horn could not believe his eyes. It was himself as he once was, long ago.

The warrior asked, "Do you remember your people when they were young and strong?"

Moose Horn shook his head. "No," he replied. "It grows harder as I grow older."

"There will be more white men on the river soon," said the warrior.

Moose Horn heard himself ask, "How many?" And the young man swept his arm across the star-filled sky. "Too many," he said. "Too many to count."

"What shall I do?" asked Moose Horn. But as suddenly as it had come, the dream was gone. All that remained was the whispering breeze, high in the ironwood trees.

Moose Horn opened his eyes. Spotted Deer stood by his side. He called out to his parents, "Mother! Father! Come quick! Grandfather has had a dream!"

His parents came fast. So did his sisters and his uncles. Soon a crowd had gathered.

Everyone waited, for they knew a dream was a gift and something to share.

"On the wind," Moose Horn began, "come Kaskaskia, Delaware, and Creek, Cherokee and Cree . . . They are being blown west by settlers and the soldiers' steel."

Moose Horn glanced around him, wanting to be sure his people understood.

"There is a man," he said, "who stands in the way of that wind— a man who might keep us from blowing away forever. He is the Medicine Painter, George Catlin."

At dawn, Moose Horn went with a small gift of tobacco among
the dark pines. He went where he thought the Great Spirit, Manito,

might listen to an old man's prayers. When he was done, he knew his spirit would reach the western sky.

Moose Horn returned to the village. He put on the purple war belt and the red sash with the eagle feather. Then he sat down for the Medicine Painter.

As the people crowded around, George Catlin asked Moose Horn to turn his face and look into the distance. "Now turn back slowly," he said, "and look at me. That's it!"

Catlin worked quickly. And when the people looked at the picture of Moose Horn, they could see that it was just as he was—with the wisdom of dreams and the courage to face the western sky.

Spotted Deer came and put his head on Moose Horn's shoulder. He touched the purple war belt. "Grandfather," he said, "you are so handsome."

And on that canvas cloth, Moose Horn would live forever.

To Anne, best of friends. A.L.

For Brock and Maj. M.deC.

I would like to thank the following for their help on this project: Jody Beaulieu, tribal archivist and director of the tribal archives and library at Red Lake Nation, Minnesota; Evan Maurer, director of the Minneapolis Institute of Arts; and Nancy Anderson, associate curator of American and British paintings at the National Gallery of Art, Washington, D.C. Special thanks to Joseph Ager, assistant director, the Pipestone County Historical Society, and David Rambow, director, the Pipestone County Museum, both in Pipestone, Minnesota, for their patience and expertise. *A.L.*

Library of Congress Cataloging-in-Publication Data

Littlesugar, Amy.
A portrait of Spotted Deer's grandfather/
written by Amy Littlesugar;
illustrated by Marlowe deChristopher.
p.   cm.
Summary: When Spotted Deer's grandfather dreams that one white man can keep the Indians from blowing away forever, Moose Horn agrees to let George Catlin paint his portrait.
ISBN 0-8075-6622-5
1. Indians of North America—Juvenile fiction. 2. Catlin, George, 1796-1872—Juvenile fiction. [1. Indians of North America—Fiction. 2. Catlin, George, 1796-1872—Fiction. 3. Artists—Fiction.]
I. deChristopher, Marlowe, ill. II. Title.
PZ7.L7362Po   1997   96-2704
[Fic]—dc20   CIP   AC

Text © copyright 1997 by Amy Littlesugar.
Illustrations © copyright 1997 by Marlowe deChristopher.
Published in 1997 by Albert Whitman & Company,
6340 Oakton Street, Morton Grove, Illinois 60053.
Published simultaneously in Canada
by General Publishing, Limited, Toronto.
Printed in the U.S.A.
10   9   8   7   6   5   4   3   2   1

The text typeface is Janson Text.
The paintings are rendered in oil.
The interior design is by Susan B. Cohn
and Karen Johnson Campbell.
The cover design is by Susan B. Cohn.